The Program Illusion

Les Cook

Published by Les Cook, 2022.

Fiction

Intended for a Mature Audience.

Revised Edition

Published: 2022

Contact: Les Cook

Lescook360@gmail.com

Library and Archives Canada:

395 Wellington Street. Ottawa ON. KIA 0N4

Printed Book ISBN 978-1-9990023-3-6

Electronic book ISBN 978-1-9867214-8-9

Table of Contents

Table of Contents

Context

Preface

———

I have no excuse or warning, only agenda – read the story.

Channel

———

YESTERDAY – TODAY.

Everything is forever on computer.

A Bulgarian is to blame for my pleasures.

I sat next to her on a bus to Prague.

She was her exotic self and I thought I would be the smart one.

She was smarter, I learnt, she taught. My eyes opened to what I couldn't perceive.

You see – I'd fallen out of love and not just the elicit kind but of life itself and all the feelings that go with a twenty-first-century being.

The Bulgarian spoke, "You must live life in two places, externally in the environment and internally in your mind." She continued, "Remember in here," her hand pointed to her head, "and here" indicating to the world. "You need both. What we think inside is true life. The outside environment is the trap or escape. Don't take the environment in first. Let the internal reach out. Listen to yourself, the thoughts the world hid for thousands of years with advertisements of their own strong beliefs."

She thinks as I, an ideologue.

What I think moves beyond my ears, or am I the willing soldier in an unannounced movement? Is this evolution?

It is a grand scheme, a puzzle of change.

A revolution without the gun.

The last thing she said was, "Meet me tonight."

I left her at that – we were supposed to meet at a synagogue in Prague.

I was late and never saw her again, it was supposed to be like that. If I'd met her the lustre wouldn't last; maybe love, maybe sex, maybe lifelong friendship, but the lustre would not be as great as myth. I will not find faults this way. My deity, I don't even remember her name. Perfect.

I was set off, nothing mattered, only pursuing what I wanted.

Motion.

Quick on the phone, the internet.

I put my house up for sale, no problem because I'd never lived in the house, only rented it out.

I wouldn't be answering the phone to return to work.

My truck up for sale too.

As much as I didn't like it, I'd have to return to Canada for some of these duties. I'd also have to pack my pockets with cash.

Bratislava, three weeks later.

A tortuous beauty.

Vienna all in a day.

When the bus arrived back in Bratislava, I entered a pub next to the guest house and drank two beers quickly while thinking about the sexy receptionist of the guest house. When I check in, the receptionist tells me of another woman "A strange girl is staying here from your country."

"Why is she strange?" I question the receptionist with whom I've developed a friendship.

"You will see. She is like you. She has stayed here before. She comes now, speak with her."

If she is like me, then she is thinking of seducing you – is what I think at the receptionist.

The buzz of the doorbell, "She is here now" speaks the receptionist.

I want to ask how she knows, but the receptionist knows all. She knows I will ask her out again until she says yes, or a sure no.

Enter Strange Girl.

She is indeed magnificently strange, everything strange isn't. From distance, a complete woman in understated clothing, makeup and manners. She wears a cap covering short hair, her skin light, her features dark, about 5 feet 8 inches tall. I can't stop looking at her actions and listening to her speech.

I ask myself why she stays in this budget guest house.

"What were you doing in Vienna?" she asks me.

"The Cézanne exhibition."

"And... what did you find?" Like there was nothing to find.

"I found an excuse to explore my art inside the art of life. I also found it sexually stimulating, a certain atmosphere."

"Living art, you live life as art." More of a hopeful statement than a question.

"I'm not an artist. My life is my art," is my response.

"I agree, you should live your life as art, to be looked upon and studied. I'm glad to have checked you out. Polite conversation angers me, it makes my heart beat; I hate the human race. Unguarded truths are victorious in my heart."

The receptionist intercedes, "Tea?"

The receptionist nods at me. Her nod says, now go fuck her, and I'll watch. I laugh; if only Strange Girl hadn't appeared, maybe me and the receptionist together?

"Where have you come from?" Strange Girl asks.

"Budapest."

"Did you find a beautiful Hungarian woman?"

I can't answer her. I ignore the question instead of speaking, remembering I can't lie. This is her test.

"What's your name?" she asks.

"L Ce." I answer.

"Hi I'm K." She answers.

Conversation advances to a sitting area where tea is served.

It is found we are both from the same part of Canada.

I explain my situation of putting my house up for sale in the hope to escape. "I'm not trying to run. I just want to create new ideals and live without the extensions of how I was raised and what I learnt."

"Where will you go?" she asks.

"I will decide that later. Right now, I'm thinking about what action I should take. I'm to go back to Canada this week. This trip is sort of a start to confirm. Goodbye to my job, forget telephone numbers, streets, emotions, feelings, love these are the things I must learn to forget."

"Interesting, so what do you believe in? You know politics, religion, philosophy?"'

"Nothing," is my reply.

"You must believe in something?"

"I believe everything inside is true and everything outside is not unless I make it true. I create from the inner to the outer environment, not the other way around. I was hindered by religion, philosophy, astronomers, futurists, governments, education, friends, and family all a created past that interrupts my future. On this trip I've come to forget about what they all say and listen to what I think and discard what I've heard. Just listen to my inside, the inside that holds every bit of the world, the world I'm a part of."

"Now what?" she questions.

"Now I've begun to create. I must empty my feelings of all I've seen, heard, read, and listened. Take emotion out of the equation, remove everything that resonates in my nerves, habits gone."

"What's your plan, suicide? Or change your name and disappear?"

"Learn – do, evolve, teach, change," I answer her.

"How?"

"My mind," is my answer.

"I can help you," she claims. "I know a place that wasn't designed for someone like you but could be altered for your needs. You could clean the toxins, the habits, develop new daily routines. Resolve the world, give yourself freedom."

I ask, "Where?"

"British Columbia, just outside Vancouver, a Spa/ Retreat," she almost giggles. "Listen, it isn't your normal spa, they have meditation, hypnosis, flotation tank, think tank, diet plan, hiking, designed detox as you like and studies. Everything a man needs to change."

"I don't need tools. All the tools that we have to provide results are already stored in our mind. I just need time and a place to devise a system of training and not the hindrance of my current life." I reply.

"Exactly – now listen to me. We can design a program. You can create a daily routine. Go stay for months."

"Who pays for this?" I question.

"Money just goes around. I'll tell them you want to erase your mind of clutter. You will have a contract. They'll catalogue, research the experience. Or is that too intrusive? Look at it as a business."

"What do you do? What do you get?" I ask her.

"I do all kinds of things. I make short movies and stories about life."

"Will I be in your movie?"

"Story – I haven't taken your picture, no movie." She laughs. "We can do promotion, a documentary, an entertaining journey with the Spa/Retreat; this is how you will pay for the time you spend there. Maybe even make money. I will take a commission for thinking and setting this up. Don't disappoint me. How do you think I travel for months at a time?"

All the specifics are hashed out late into the night.

Strange Girl makes contact and discusses the program with the Spa/Retreat.

It sounds like a scheme. If I'm so passionate about change, why should I turn it into a show for profit?

I take her motives as affection, some inner compulsion to please me.

The next day I don't see her until the evening when she knocks at my door.

She speaks, "I will wake you in the morning and we can go to Prague."

She's in nightwear, her cap gone. Silk lingerie, and black stockings on. A lean body with baby fat amongst glorious strong bones. Her finger flirts with the strap of her green brassiere before she walks out of the door.

Once in Prague she informs me she'll be catching a train to Berlin the next morning. I will catch a flight to Amsterdam and then on to the Spa/Retreat in Canada. More details, correspondence between me her and the Spa/Retreat – by evening I'm exhausted, sad, happy.

Everything is set.

A knock at my door.

Strange Girl is in sexy blue jeans and a loose sparkling shirt that shows off her muscled shoulders.

Before I have a chance to say hello her lips are on mine, a subtle sensual kiss that I've never experienced before. She kisses intensely well. A kiss this sweet personifies just how gorgeously strange she is. Her hands soothe my body as we back farther into the room until we are suddenly stopped by the edge of a desk.

She stops the kiss.

Shakes her head – and says, "How I want to but you would not be able to erase your mind of me and your experiment would be all about me. My lips say yes but my heart says no. My mind, what does my mind say?"

"Your mind says shut the door."

"Yes – my mind says shut the door and say goodbye."

She backs up, walks out. The door is shut.

I count to 9 and follow.

She is gone.

I knock on her door, no answer.

I look outside and cannot see her. I ask the front desk, no answer, I wait late into the night for her sound, nothing is heard.

In the morning she is gone. She's left the key in the room, not a trace of her.

I wander over to the train station and search the platform for Berlin.

I can't find her.

I erase her from my brain after I dream about fucking her.

I haven't heard from her since and won't ask about her at the Spa/Retreat.

In Vancouver – I'm picked up at the airport by a pretty young woman with extreme large eyes who says she is to be one of my assistants. I sign papers, agreements. I spend two weeks as a guest at a mountain lodge before I enter a room at the Spa/ Retreat that will be my home for how long? I don't know; more than three months less than nine. Time won't be kept. I may record time, but I won't have a clock. It is now year-end 1999. My house is left in the hands of a real estate agency to take care of, they will send papers if the house is sold.

The Retreat

———

DOCTOR PAUL LOUIS GREETS me. "Welcome back to the real world."

I'm relaxing on a futuristic astronaut chair in my kung fu apparel specifically designed for me.

Welcome, it is what the raven said when I hiked on the mountain behind The Retreat I stay. When the raven sang – the song came from inside my body. "Welcome," my body said to the outside world and not the outside world to me. I'm already here, the world isn't.

Thank you raven, I've discovered what I thought and once thought, through my eyes it goes out to the world.

"How long have I been here?" I ask the doctor.

"Almost seven months." The doctor smiles, "How do you feel?"

"Like a sex crazed maniac."

"The assistants?" the doctor responds.

"Yes," I answer.

I have three assistants, three treasures on different shifts. An androgynous-looking assistant who has my sexual mind most days, a voluptuous assistant that loves to flirt, and a perfect assistant with large eyes I enjoy without sexual thoughts.

"It is a conspiracy to keep us here." The doctor laughs.

"Can I stay?" I joke.

Doctor Paul Louis is the only male contact I have here at The Retreat. The doctor is not a tall man, he's brawny, good-looking in his late thirties. He carries his hair sheltering one eye permitting his straight nose to jut out.

Paul Louis speaks, "Don't relax too much; you have a busy day today. Your first day will be hard on the brain."

"The first day of my second life," I comment.

"You don't miss your first life?"

"I miss my life here at The Retreat."

"You miss your time here and you haven't even left?" he suggests.

"I miss what you call imagination. My imagination has been as real as us here now."

"You've survived in your imagination." The doctor thinks.

"I didn't survive, I lived – I'd survived before I entered The Retreat – I survived my past. My past before this experiment is nothing but a photo album. My history is trivial messages."

The doctor interrupts, "We don't have much time to talk – you have to move into your new room before your visitors come to see you."

"Visitors from my imagination?"

"No," he chuckles. "A beautiful woman and your parents, many people would like to see you but you have only allowed these people."

"My girlfriend of my first life is beautiful?" I ask excitedly.

"Yes, a lovely girl."

The doctor and I talk several times a month, not on a schedule I can figure out, that is the trick of the experiment. I suppose he checks my vital signs, my brain, he oversees that I'm not going to die on The Retreat premises.

I'd agreed to have visitors before I entered The Retreat. I couldn't just say goodbye to my parents and girlfriend without at least a personal visit. I thought it best after my stint in the program to say goodbye as opposed to before it. No likes or dislikes. Capitalism or communism I like nothing I haven't a favourite – I am clean of thought, everything I've been taught lost, I can't say learned if lost.

"What is the real world, outside or in here?" I ask Doctor Paul Louis.

"I don't know," he answers. "I spend too much time in here, and not enough out there. Work that one enjoys and money is all that matters, or is it? What would do say?"

"I'd say, do what feels good, wherever and whatever it may be. Do what you must even if it doesn't feel good for a short time."

Mel the voluptuous blonde assistant enters to guide me to my new room. Mel swings my cock today, but still, it is the androgynous-looking assistant that has my mind while the doctor is consumed by mind and body with the perfect assistant with extremely large eyes, their eyes can't lie when they are together.

Doctor Paul Louis says we can go out for a drink when I finish my time. He says he's separated from his wife, no children. I've been teasing him for months about going out to find women together.

Mel escorts me to my new room – what fabulous hips she has in her uniform. The Retreat has the sexiest uniforms for the assistants, though they are not uniforms at all, outfits matching and mismatching, jackets and pullovers accenting short collared buttoned shirts, soft slacks with a loose fit. Oh, if ever there was one assistant who would break the rules, it would be Mel. The assistants essentially do their tasks without communication, purposely ignoring me. Androgynous is the best at this, she's dangerously visual in my sexual fantasies but doesn't give me the time of day, she performs her task quite well though. It is Mel who forgets and talks shop. Even the doctor refuses to break down and open up even though I can see he'd enjoy talking about almost anything with me.

I find my new room.

I wish Mel's hips could stay with me "Come in, shut the door," I tell her.

"We don't have time – you have visitors." She smiles.

"Are they here now?"

"Yes outside."

"They can wait."

"They will have to wait a long time."

"You are that good?"

"Maybe," she smiles walking away. "My shift is over, bye."

I'm supposed to be a gentleman – it is one of the things I've been working on, but I'm so happy today. The room is much smaller than my secluded retreat room though this room has a small fridge with vegetables inside. When in retreat I'd order my meal and drinks a couple of days in advance. I was given literature that told me exactly what I ate, drank, allowing no alcohol or drugs including prescription unless, of course, it was unavoidable. I would get out hike in the mountain trails behind The Retreat. No TV. Music played if I switched sound on. I'd asked not to read books, though some reading was provided. Sometimes I'd write and mostly I'd sit, stretch, roll around on the floor and think inside my mind. After a while, I'd sleep a little and then write, go out for a hike, read some information about the human body, the human mind or food. Think about the universe. They didn't tell me when my meals would come, they came in no particular order. I'm on video most times, doesn't bother me. Only entrances and the middle of rooms are monitored, I have lots of personal space. I laughed in retreat because I knew I was being watched, getting paid, fantastic; give them a show. I could have stayed forever if my assistants sexed me, I guess I could have requested this also.

My visitors walk in – it is nothing.

Heartless swung at Mom and Dad, they could be anyone's parents, they say they're mine.

I'm polite, and when a woman walks into my room as my former girlfriend what can I say but "how are you" did I really fall in love with her? The doctor said beautiful. She's my age, pleasant-looking not tall or short, a nice smile, but love? Couldn't be love, maybe routine? A hug I don't want it, no emotion. I want to hold the androgynous-looking assistant who now waits just out the door, I want to leave this place with her now, come Androgynous let me lick your tits and stay inside an hour... she's so light, strong.

Joking by my father, caring by my mother, happy is my past girlfriend.

Okay a five-minute visit by my parents and my former girlfriend, they'll be back again tomorrow. It is true I've done it, no feelings, I've forgotten loved ones. I wonder why I'd fallen in love with my past girlfriend. Was there nothing left between me and her except keep, jealousy, children, cheating, or forget?

My parents and ex were told not to talk of current events, past events. All the information I'm to receive of family, friends, illness, wealth, poverty, break-ups and romances can be done in the future if I so dare. They've been told to tell people what I'm doing. I've gone to a Spa/Retreat for intensive meditation.

I don't feel sadness in my heartlessness. They may feel like victims of my experiment but really, I'm the victim of life we all are.

Next, I see the Director of The Retreat, Karen Winters.

She has a receptionist, but I don't have to wait.

The entrance of her office is grand with a courtyard. Warm or cold, she gets out. The radio is blaring.

Karen in heels watching her weight in fantastic outfits, usually skirts and a blouse. A strong face, wouldn't say cute, good features, complete and clean, no outrageous blemishes, with lines of spoil and conditioning for a woman in her forties.

"What time did you come in this morning, Karen?"

"I stayed here last night. I was up at four and working at five."

"Why so busy?"

"Overseas calls, and you, lots to arrange for you. You are a full-time job."

"I bet you were too," I suggest.

"I still am," she smiles. "Tell me about your visit with your girlfriend and parents?"

"You could see it on the monitor."

"I can't see inside your head."

"Read about it, watch it, I'll write poetry about it in my daily report. For one thing, I don't have a girlfriend and my parents are just people I've met with. The world has just started, the past is nothing, I haven't an emotion."

"Is that the way you feel?"

"I don't have feelings. All I know is now and the imaginary life I've been living here at The Retreat. You see, my life in my mind is real, and now in a few days when I leave here, I'll create something new."

"So the experiment was a success. We here at The Retreat did our job."

I pretend not to listen.

Instead, I ask. "Karen, what happens next?"

"Next you will meet the person whom you'll assist for three months."

"Assist?"

"Yes, you will travel and assist Cassandra with her work and our experiment – it is a joint venture between us and her."

"Who is Cassandra and what does she do?"

"Sometimes she's working on a book. Sometimes she's a photographer, a video artist, and most times she's searching for confusion."

"And I'll assist her for that?"

"I wouldn't talk. She's doing a study and documenting it."

"Are you sure she's not a con artist? What's the study on?"

"Her study is on you for one and the rest I don't understand. I will tell you this; she takes this art of confusion very seriously. If you don't like or agree with what she's doing, she won't mind. That is part of her thing, confusion. I'm confused trying to explain it and she'll confuse you when she explains it to you."

"That's how she does it, complete confusion."

"Exactly, she confused The Retreat into recommending her research and we went as far to say we'd be interested in her work."

"Research in what?" I ask.

"She wants to send a message to the planet and requires an assistant who can share ideal theories and who hasn't preconceived notions. You think that's the task, thinking."

"And assist."

"Assist in thinking, writing, travel, decisions, shooting video, interviews, fun stuff. You'll be a part of something. I don't know what, but a part of something. You'll be flying somewhere overseas. It may be immediate or in a few days after the interview, so be prepared. The interview is in two days at the airport."

"I guess I have to fulfill my contract."

"Yes, and it will be fun to roam with Cassandra."

"I'm ready now," I answer smothered in excited wonder.

"You will need clothing for your interview with Cassandra. A designer is coming, no pressure, just try her. She designed the kung fu outfits and hiking clothing you wear."

"I haven't money."

"Just sign her bill and we will pay for it off your account. I asked the designer to come this afternoon."

I walk out of Karen's office thinking I don't know the year 2000.

The Designer

———

"MY NAME IS NADIA – I have come to give you clothing."

I don't know where she is from. I like her, her accent, she is complete living sexuality.

She is impossible, an impossible woman to have – so lovely.

She may be the height of my former girlfriend with wider hips, hair that is long and curly. Her skin is a dark sandy shade, her blood is from Asia. She wears a light, long shawl. Her thumbs and nails are hard, fingers scraped and tattered. She speaks in pauses; that is to say, she not only stops between sentences but in mid-word. She speaks, reflects, and continues with partial words and word endings. Nadia holds the listener hostage in a belief that each word she speaks is precise for the meaning conveyed. I think this is the language of choice and used by many, a form of vocal art that's swept the nation. It isn't, I know this woman is original. Nadia is genuine human art.

She has clothing for me already made and patterns in the progress of being made.

Nadia speaks, "You have complete control of what I do."

How she lies – she has control of my clothing, my look. I don't fight her. She made the kung fu like outfit I wear now.

"C-a-n I give you a suit jacket – for when it is cold? A sweater under the jacket for when it is colder. A shirt for when it is warm – pants to match the jacket – sweater, and shirt?"

I say, "Yes," to everything.

She continues, "Maybe... I will make you two shirts, two colours. This is all I have time for. I'll have to buy a sweater. I would like to invite you to my shop to try on the outfit, it would be easier. Can you come?"

I can no longer hear her pause in speech, one long pause that descends my spine and lifts.

"I'd like this," I answer.

"I will talk to Karen."

Nadia has taken my size.

She begins to design on the table of my room.

She designs deep in her mind. And when her meditation is broken, she talks joyous.

Struck – I've been struck hard with a wardrobe by a woman I never expected. My assistants have left my sexual lust. Nadia will be thought tonight.

To sleep, and even that I can't do – months of sleeping for short periods as I liked have left me with short stints of deep sleep.

Morning, my parents are at my door before I can shower.

Mother pushes questions and father is reserved.

My former girlfriend says goodbye like nothing has changed. I think she thinks only time stops us from returning to the way we were – as if I'm gone off to work for a few months.

"Don't wait," I'd like to speak, but I'm not in a present mind to even consider there ever was us.

When they are gone, I have no one to report to, it is like I'm again in retreat except this day, I wait to leave.

Nadia the designer arrives in the afternoon.

It is true I have done nothing today but wait for her.

She cleverly disguises beauty.

She is a statue veiled, today she sheds.

My eyes sparkle.

Nadia is the exact opposite of a typical model but frighteningly sensual, an attractiveness I hadn't fully noticed until she shed her shawl to reveal a body boasting of full curves in a halter and jeans. Her beauty is a seductive weapon she has suspended and freed as a personal gift. Tightness strangles us, a tightness only two strangers can have. Pulsating blue, the heat will not be turned down between us till we explode together.

Shirt, slacks, shoes – though she won't let me see them.

Instead, "Take off your pants," she demands.

I do.

She hands me attire. I pull up new slacks. With her help, I put on a collared shirt.

"I love this outfit. To see it on you is very good."

A jacket pattern is put on and then taken off. A sweater on and then jacket pattern again. Last, with slight touch she guides on shoes.

"I did bring you one present," she passes me some very casual clothing.

"Throw it away if you like."

"I would never throw away anything you give me."

Before she leaves Nadia says, "I can't keep a secret. Will you come see me at my shop? I have asked Karen and she said 'yes' if you like. My shop closes at 5:30 so knock on the door loud and I will let you in at 5:35."

In a fast strike, she kisses me on the lips.

I haven't time to react even though it is a slow kiss done quickly.

"Okay." She looks to escape as fast as she's kissed.

I take her hand to stop and turn her back towards me.

"Ah," she screams in laughter and presses her hand hard into mine. "Bye," she says. I won't let her go – "Noooo!" she pleads joyfully. She laughs and points, "Camera."

I relent, bid goodbye.

She is my hunger and has my full attention.

Karen the director summons me soon after.

"Have you accomplished to forget your past?" Karen asks.

"Yes – no emotion with the past.'

"And how long will it last?"

'Forever – I will develop new feelings for family and friends as I get to know them. History is something recorded. I haven't recorded anything, foods, games, habits, loyalties, religion, culture, clean the world has no history, no universe, I will learn everything now, right or wrong, grade one."

"Your time here was kindergarten?" Karen asks.

"No, the womb – and my days since have been kindergarten."

"You may become the same as before?"

"There is no before, only imagination," I answer.

"Nadia stopped in to see me, you can go see her after you meet with Cassandra at the airport. I will give you your driver's license, we have rented a car for you. This will be your last night here at The Retreat, when you are finished in three months you can stay here for a week if you like to get resettled."

"Thank you, anything else?" I question.

"You can go and we will capture all your information through Cassandra. I will see you when you come back. You are free."

She smiles in my eyes as if a crush has spoken.

I've never thought of sex with Karen – but now at this minute I could.

I could kiss her, and she wouldn't stop me. She hugs me and walks to her window. I say goodbye, walk back to my room.

The doctor comes to my door soon after.

"Tomorrow evening, can you meet me? Karen said you'll be visiting the city. If you have any problems I can try and help. The past may begin to gnaw. Others find it difficult when confronted with their past. It may not be as easy as you think on the outside. The future usually becomes one's past. It is a circular life. I hope you will come see me in the evening; we can have a nice time away from this place not working. I can only work in this place, and you can only follow your curriculum. Come tomorrow night, I've written down the address and time."

The past hasn't begun to gnaw, as the doctor suggested.

Officially The Spa/Retreat is said to be a place of alternate thinking, meditation and extensive relaxation. Karen will say I had all the answers I needed before I entered The Retreat, it's not her fault I can't remember the answers or didn't ask the questions. My experiment is confidential for the time being as are others, "We do many things, some people just come to relax like staying at a spa" as Karen will say. Up the mountain they do have hot springs they use, so technically it could be a spa, it certainly is a retreat. I don't know what they learn, teach, sell, make themselves money, I guess. All the questions I didn't care before are now coming to air, and still, I don't care. The outside environment I don't control, I only have control of my interior.

Strange Girl

———

THE AIRPORT FOR MY interview.

Beethoven's Moonlight Sonata spins backwards in my head. Methodical I sit. A girl confounded in thought walks near, dark brown bangs crisscross her face. The bangs clipped at her neck. The bangs are placed behind her ears. Pissing medication is the impression she gives. She's in a light blue synthetic jacket and black loose-fitting pants. She's pushing a luggage cart. The cart is parked near me.

"Can you watch this for me?" is spoken by her.

"Yes," I answer.

She returns untamed, her jacket off, a leopard print on, low-cut, bare skin. A book dug from her bag, reading begins. Self-imposed encouragement . . . my mouth opens, transactions begin. The water is warm, normal questions fly back and forth. My imagination sees us close in the sun. She has a few hours before her flight.

I ask softly, "Would you like to join me outside in the sun?"

"Let's go." She answers.

I recognize her. As she walks, I realize what is happening.

She is Strange Girl of my past, and now she is Cassandra of my present future.

"How long was it going to take you," she laughs. "My name is Cassandra."

I remember her, the emotions are new – a stranger she still is, an exciting stranger.

"You have a new name. Or I didn't know your name and now I do."

"Cassandra is my full name – Prophet of Disaster."

"I don't understand?"

"Cassandra means prophet of disaster, my mother's idea. I don't like to call myself Cassandra but now that you know, go ahead and call me Cassandra instead of K. My mother named me Cassandra, if my mother likes something, she goes with it."

I nod in understanding.

A fantastic shock. My world is most unusual – engrossed in solitude I haven't thought of her.

I follow her legs, blood rushes up my skin as we pass by benches, people.

"Let's go to the end." She sends.

The path swerves – more people, more benches.

The end, we come to the end. Her breast prompt, waving, she stretches, her lips wet, I marvel as she sunbaths, she's caught me watching. She speaks, "The Retreat wouldn't give me details... so tell me about yourself?"

"What you see is what is known," I answer abrasively.

"Why would you say that?"

"Because nothing is to know," I state.

"So you are dead, ha, ha, ha."

Her head deep to her knees in humour, steady again she glares to my face with streaks of hair about her mouth. "I'm sorry, do you hate me? Your story is just too funny, you're too funny. I do like your slacks and shirt. Where did you get them?"

"They were made for me and given at the Spa/Retreat."

"How old are you?"

"Thirty something, thirty-two I guess."

"Did you miss a year somewhere? You are thirty-three, turning thirty-four" again laughing. "Do you know how old I am?"

"Did I ever know?"

"I'm twenty-one or twenty-two, no, that was last year. I'm twenty-three." She laughs. "So tell me what have you been doing at The Retreat? Forgetting your past, or making up a future?"

She dangles me from a rope, dripping water droplets one at a time.

"Back to nature," I speak.

"You think you can survive in the woods?"

All my energy is swayed to confidant speech.

"Nope – it isn't about the woods it is about the universe and the human."

"Are you sure it wasn't about free lodging?"

Her remarks, facial expressions have sobered me. I've become sullen, introverted, soft words and expressionless motion has lent to a slouch. She's picked up on my shell.

"Will you assist me in dismantling the world?" She asks with a more positive stroke.

"If you like," I answer.

Her voice now tender and movements slight caring, "Listen I'm glad that you've agreed to come and assist me, assist is a bad word I don't know what role you'll play other than yourself and what you've become. I haven't much money to give you but we will live well and do important things. I will give you a credit card for emergencies. What more do you want in life besides all the money to do what you like?"

"Are you working for them, The Retreat?" I ask, soft-spoken.

"I have for my selfish self, it's all for me, everything I do, no matter what someone may think. So the answer is no." A long reflective pause, "I should go wait at my gate. Will you come?"

"Where?"

"Do you have to know? Just look in your passport and see if you can figure it out."

"I don't have my passport."

"Sorry. I have it – take it. Here is your e-mail and password. Here is my e-mail, come find me. Here is your airplane ticket."

We make our way to her gate whereupon she stops and states. "Listen, don't create any misconceptions of romance. You've been asleep the last seven months. I understand your needs. You'll have plenty of opportunities on your own as will I. I have to go now." She stops turns and speaks, "You will come, won't you?"

I open the ticket – Budapest. "Yes," I answer.

I refuse to look inside my passport.

I drive to the Designers shop.

Nadia lets me in.

Material is strewn wall to wall, really a disgrace, sewing machines cluttered amongst paper and fabric, large mirrors in dust.

Nadia is alone as she shuts off the entry lights, "I don't want anybody knocking."

I'm not nervous – I should be but I'm not. That is the trick of the dynamic Nadia – she makes me comfortable.

In the off-coloured dim light, a goddess whispers "I'd like to speak 'close your eyes' though I can't speak like this. Can try your outfit?"

"Yes."

She wears a dark purple wrap that traverses her body held by three silver buttons, perfume and cryptic makeup. Nadia is undetectable.

"Undress, I will return with your clothing."

We kiss.

Almost naked and exposed to cold, a cold I desire and beg for her to touch and speak warmth.

A smooth smouldering shirt is first, light and cool. She laces down my legs, her hair tingles my mid-drift slacks are slithered up.

Nadia's hands on my shirt seams, each rib counted, a jacket is placed.

"Look in the mirror," she commands.

On a look I see a stranger and alongside this stranger are the silver buttons of Nadia reflected, then released as her clothing is softly laid to the floor.

I follow; undo what I've just put on.

Clever we face each other.

Our fur shivers.

Trembling like virgins we blend on the table.

Juicing serpents, on waves we ride like swans.

High.

Extraordinarily slow we move, talk, touch, make love.

"Do you like the suit?" she asks.

"I do."

"In three months, I'll sell this pattern to the world. No one is brave enough to wear your suit yet. After you stalk the world men and women will be brave enough to patronize this outfit. Only you can wear this clothing now."

It is getting late – we both speak the same, we don't want to stop this night but we have to.

Both our necks low, I resist temptation and dress. She leaves to another room.

Now that I can see myself in the clothing alone, I see peculiar. I'm suited for the apparel, rough, exotic. She's pulled off the impossible; I'd never select this clothing myself to wear – on me it has an interesting look.

Nadia returns with her clothing and a jacket on.

"I have to lock up. You can walk me down the street?"

We walk and I don't expect anything.

She instructs, "Don't speak – just hold me."

I don't speak words.

I hear her say, "You can't see me – I can't see you – I'm to be married soon."

Her hand folds her hair back, her mouth open, her engagement ring shining. She holds me long enough for no further advance. She enters her car and drives away.

There is no need to chase and there is no use to cry, I'm living more than I'd dreamed. I've overcome the phobia of life.

It is a wonder that the best is only seen for a few moments of life and this is why it is called the best – unattainable.

I drive to meet the doctor.

A pleasant place, the lounge though spacious is quaint with private tables.

Each table is positioned with a barrier, a sort of personal touch.

The lounge has a nice assortment of people.

I sit at the bar and think about having a drink.

"A strong beverage may put you under the table," Doctor Paul Louis voices.

"It may," I answer.

The doctor is at a table behind and motions for me to join him. He wears an upbeat navy-blue suit. He looks well, important and handsome, his hair greased down.

"You have your new suit, very nice." He compliments me. "Cranberry juice or red wine with a flask of water?" the doctor asks.

"That sounds good, wine with a flask of water, and yourself?"

"I like to drink scotch, not too much a couple of glasses, double on ice, then a single with water to finish the night, so I don't find myself under the table."

The waitress isn't some barmaid but a ripe dignified nymph.

"Not many people know of this palace, it is a gem that is far from the circuit. It is a club without the stuffiness. Do you want to join?" he laughs as he can see my attention cruising, marking the nymph who serves.

"Yes," I exclaim. Still euphoric I haven't anything else to say. A woman has never raped me with her eyes before the way this ripe dignified nymph does.

The doctor speaks, "I envy you. I live through you in fantasy, I emulate you."

"You do, do you," nonchalant in my answer.

Paul Louis finishes his drink in a gobble, "Because it is you who has changed my life, I wasn't happy. And when you told me about making a change and doing what you feel, I thought 'yes' and now to see you do it is tremendous. I don't know how you met Karen, yet I do because you made it happen. You instigated an incident to solve a situation. Somehow you gather energy that isn't scientific . . . you accumulate sources you need to accomplish what you can. No not what you can but what you must. Courageous, you are courageous."

"I think you're overstating luck." I taste my wine with a slurp.

"Sometimes I think I should quit The Retreat. This brain galvanizing isn't for me it's for her."

"Who's her?" I ask.

"Karen. It's nothing to me." His right eyebrow is raised. "It's all Karen's. She persuaded me to join her three and half years ago. It isn't my dream. I was in love with Karen. I'm still in love with Karen... it may not be love now, infatuation. We visited each other romantically for two years. I left my wife for her. And she hasn't had anything to do with me since. I've made good money – and I like my job, but it wasn't supposed to be like this. It isn't too late though I can change my life as you did." After a moment of reflection, he adds insignificantly "Karen laughs when I date other women."

"So it's Karen's Spa/Retreat, she owns it?" I question.

"Karen's invention. She is an amazing woman. She doesn't have a degree, only in bullshit. When she was young she married an older man. An older man with money – he has since passed away. She opened The Retreat four years ago. She lured me in, gave me a nice position and we've guided it into the success that it is today."

"Why did she want The Retreat?"

"Her own screening room . . . games of the eccentric, the study of people. A detox spa. A meditation spa. A change of life retreat. She is funded. You are her darling. You're what she's been waiting for. Karen is an incredible woman. I must live the truth and escape her clutches."

"What about your wife, do you still love your wife?"

"I always loved my wife. I'm too embarrassed to see her, to talk to her, to admit I'm Karen's. My wife knows I'm a fool. I can't live like that. I will live two lives, as you will. She loves you Karen does. A woman like Karen doesn't fall in love as we do . . . she's too smart for that. She's done all this for you. Do you know how much a procedure like you've asked for costs? And she's giving you money on top of the costs to live a dream life. People would line up around the corner if they could forget their past, take a vacation at a spa and start a new life and be paid for it. How have you managed this?"

The dignified nymph brings the doctor another drink.

"I have a woman waiting for me, a cocktail girl if you may. What about this cocktail girl who serves us? Are you interested in her?" He refers to the dignified nymph.

"Very – but not tonight."

"My wife is an attractive rather ordinary woman, intelligent though. I was happy with her and knew what to expect, there weren't many surprises and stability prevailed. I sought Karen for excitement, torment and surprises, which brings me here. With the same cocktail girl for the past three months, stability again. Karen has dated other men while seeing me, so what's the difference? Truth, the cocktail girl's lies are truth and Karen's truths are lies. With Karen, my mind was muddled with her daily, nightly. With the cocktail girl my mind is clear, only exhilaration persists."

The evening has ended with the doctor leaving with his cocktail girl.

I shut the door to my hotel room.

My second life has begun full force . . . my mind in chaos trying to manipulate scenarios. The mind will answer questions anyway it likes. A door opens to unusual lines, dark rooms of the brain are switched on and previously dormant cells have a wealth of ancient stories. The regular string of blood rush is stumped in solitude and unmapped paths are taken. Welcome the Amazon, the Gobi Desert, and the barren Arctic.

I open my passport and see visas for Romania, Syria, Pakistan, and China.

Travel

———

CASSANDRA SPEAKS. "WHAT did you see?"

"Sunflower seeds," I answer.

"Can I record your voice?" she asks.

Moments . . . her position focused . . . my frame standing. Termination to the sorting of my luggage, attention to what Cassandra is about to speak.

"I like the way you talk. This is my art – sound, vision, print. True conversation is the thoughts we never say. So converse, say what you truly think."

I do.

"Women I won't touch can't smile. Art – legs. I loved it when I crossed the border from Hungary to Romania. Begging, foreign, not proper, not conditioned. Invincibility gone, fragility on, I want to learn why. What's the name of that fine clear Czech beer? Thoughts . . . I went out for a walk this morning, I was hungry but I couldn't eat, I couldn't order food. I ate here at the hotel. I miss a Bulgarian girl, she said incredible things, my brain worked."

"Good – very good, exactly – I didn't expect you to speak like this, but you speak well."

All inhibitions have fled. Cassandra brightens with each word she hears. We are extreme personalities in grace – Beethoven has surrendered, poets are awake.

"You're tired, you've been up early, and I know you came in very late." She acts concerned.

"Yes, but I'm happy, I'm happy I've made it here, I like this place, the high ceilings, art and wide halls. I could stay here. This is the kind of pension I'd romanticized."

I stand as a possessed man stoned on another planet . . . no recollections of earth. My jacket draped over a chair, luggage scattered, socks soaking, speak if she dare.

Still, Cassandra holds underlying anger.

She comments, "I thought you might have arrived a day or two later."

"No – from Budapest I caught a taxi to the Romanian border."

"Why didn't you stay over in Budapest and catch the morning train?"

"I wanted to spend the day here."

"So you didn't spend any time in Budapest?"

"No," I answer.

"Really, I'm surprised. Budapest is amazing with beautiful women. You didn't see an exotic woman in Budapest?"

I don't respond, her words are air.

"You must return."

I understand; it has started the experiment or the performance has begun.

"I'm hungry." I Intercede.

"Let's go," she takes my hand, I release quickly.

Cassandra's legs have shell shocked me. A scent like a stem to a bloom, fragrance in a slim curved bottle of perfume, all looks until the top is unlocked and opened. She doesn't believe in a single thing, not democracy or her mind, only games.

My muscles, my stretch, I'm in a haze, my body cohesive in accordance with extreme concentration, I walk in thought, never once considering the steps I'm taking. Cassandra has never been in a haze. She's calculating, studying, and seldom dreaming, always developing. She's in a race, understanding every minute in life has reason. Cassandra doesn't kill time she captures it, destroying impressions of the popular culture to be entertained.

We sit have lunch then stroll.

Cassandra speaks harshly in a pleasant tongue; "My skin is light, my eyes dark and my hair isn't even black, I dye it, and today I need to dye as my brown hair has crept in. I'm of Northern and Southern European ancestry. I'm a monster first world person, Caucasian so I can't make fun of anyone but the world can make fun of me. I'm writing a book about you, a man. I can't write what I don't know, we'll travel and you will be my source of information. We'll make videos that will become small movies, snapshots of life. My tape recorder will add sounds to images, still and moving."

"Not first class," I mention.

"Correct. First class is only a tool to manipulate inferior, and that isn't the element I want. This is my story, my fiction, my philosophy. My world, what we think at the places and of the people we visit. We won't judge, we'll say what we feel, truth not construction. Right or wrong, it will be how and what we feel. It's not about the place or people, it is about us."

"Writing is the earth's greatest weapon. I also thought the greatest art, the most dangerous art. The pen is the devil's art," I conclude.

"You don't believe in the devil, there is no such thing. Did you forget what you are supposed to believe?"

"I haven't written the devil off yet," I confide.

"Or Jesus; don't start looking for him now, you've done this your whole life. Don't repeat yourself." She swears.

"I suppose you're right."

"You suppose I'm right? You will look for your own words and then create new ones. Like you, I'm Christian whether I like it or not, a habit hard to break since I was young. The bible is still law. For you, it is different, you are starting fresh you shouldn't have to answer to the bible, you believe in nothing."

Late in her room . . . perfume, casual discourse, she's only looking to come close to touching. I analyzing, timid to approach, I crash to sleep honestly. I think she contemplates at my side the remainder of the night – dramatization, scrutinizing sentences and actions of the day . . . confusion, heat, and moist she waits wondering why I haven't touched her.

She is cranky the next day and naps on the train.

I dream with scenery.

Women with wooden sticks in hanging bags about their shoulder walking the railway lines . . . a boy black with coal and children so sweet I wonder what happens to those eyes of life with age.

The kindest mothers blow kisses.

Cabbage rolls in Brasov, she selects for me in French.

"I wasn't sure how you'd feel about coming to Romania, homosexuality is risky here," she says with a smirking flirt.

"I'm not a homosexual," I laugh.

"Just kidding with you, but seriously how do you feel about a country where a person can't show off passion?"

"It isn't my passion; I can follow my passion here so I'm unaffected."

"What if I was affected by it?" she questions.

"Are you?" my fork up, looking for a straight answer.

"I'm not gay but let's say I was. How would you feel then?" She looks to her plate, shielding a grin.

"I would say it would be fascinating, intriguing, for you to follow your passion behind closed doors. Romantic, risky, lovely, and sexy, I would hold you in high esteem if you succeeded in exploring your passion here."

"As opposed to?" direct she contests.

"As opposed to being boring, lost, and ordinary in your own place where you can do as you like."

"The world is my place."

She settles down to dine on her potatoes. Much silence as we walk home, I'm uncomfortable, awkward. Still, I insist and proceed to let my arm comfort her shivering shoulder. In haste, her shoulder twists and her neck aim's a face with a snarl instead of grace.

"Not every woman who seems cold is asking for comfort," she hoots a laugh to herself. "Are you trying to prove something?"

A predicament . . . my timing must be perfect or I'll never succeed in what she desperately wants, I can't be clumsy, I must sweep her, ravage her gently unexpectedly.

In my silence, she relents, "I'm sorry. We have to do our work first and foremost."

The train to Bucharest . . . mountains . . . oil wells.

Almost a scratch in her eye, red veins drizzle, tired eyes the blood whistles.

With a tone in which I know the answer I speak, "Have I done a good job in assisting you with your work?"

She answers, "You understand now. When it happens, it will happen; we can't do anything to promote it, we've sent out our flyers to the world, and now we're in receptive mode. It isn't a travel story or a journal, nor is it real life. It is what it will be. We have to let the movie find us. I only know a story, images, and a voice will come. We will make music. You and I are a story. In three months, you will know me better than anyone on this earth. Remember our work is fiction, our external lives aren't real."

It is like that . . . we travel in silence as others have joined our cabin, only sly remarks are said, cheeky laughter and jokes only the two of us laugh. The rest of the people are objects placed.

In Bucharest nothing has changed, another home stay. I can't get close.

On to Istanbul we go.

We bus through Bulgaria. "Do you always live alone?" I ask.

"I experiment with people; I like to find people who'll experiment with me."

"So I'm an experiment?" I question.

"As am I, I'm yours and you are mine. All my experiments in my life have been in preparation for you and an experiment like this." She laughs, screams, "I take that back I sound. . ." more laughing. "Have I scared you?"

"No, I understand, I feel the same."

As deep as these sentences may seem the conversation doesn't intensify, we sleep sans touch, seat by seat on the overnight bus to Istanbul.

We exit groggy in the early morning.

Lali, Istanbul. Fur coats on sale, Russians dine at noon. We walk on from our hotel to the centre of tourism.

"You know we're surrounded by mosques and former churches." Cassandra motions looking forward at the Blue Mosque and sideways at The Eye of Sophia.

"I won't enter." I don't look at the mosques I look at the Japanese girls taunted by well-dressed Turkish boys.

"No, is that a promise? You won't be much of a tourist," Cassandra comments.

"Things may change."

"And temples and synagogues?" she asks as she arches her back. She knows her long back and brilliant rib cage is as much a weapon as any other part of her body.

"The same, I won't enter," I state looking away to the entrance of Sophia.

"Let's spend some time apart, what do you think?" She states as her arm lifts to the air and plants on my back.

"In what way? Different hotels or different cities?" I turn to her.

"Countries, different countries, you go to Georgia, Christian you know. Find your Jesus Christ. Spend a week away. You have to be quick because you have to make it through the Karakoram Pass before the snow. You go, you go alone and write down everything you know."

Gone are Cassandra's full lips, baby fat, and striking ribs, I'm at the door of the bus that's to curve along the Black Sea coast.

Two Turkish girls chatting in my direction.

I'm prone, alone, they attack slow but direct.

English is spoken by both.

The bus fuels up, one of the girls is taking my bus, and my attention is shifted to her, relief from constant contemplation of Cassandra.

The girl sits with an elderly lady in traditional dress. The bus is a half empty.

The girl's head swivels to meet mine, speaking kind. She's nineteen years of age. As the bus exits the city limits, she shuffles seats to be directly in front of me. Shiny clothing a modern hood, enticing, dramatic, she's evolving towards gorgeous the more I look.

We invent games so our hands can touch – strokes of sensuality, intimacies, her inability to dislodge the drapes of her window, my hand to guide. We're attracting attention.

A dinner break, I try to distance myself.

Her intense visual command brings me near.

We make future blurts and flirt.

Too much flagrant passion, attention exerts.

A male bus attendant who serves tea on the bus moves close.

The attendant sits behind listening to our words. As night approaches the attendant becomes obnoxious, insulting scolding, "Turn your light off go to sleep!"

I continue to wink; I'll seduce her now on this bus.

The attendant's temper flares, "If you don't stop talking, you will have to go sleep at the back of the bus!"

With the lights off, my hand sneaks between our seats, we hold hands we whisper.

The attendant can hear our banter he rushes to turn on my light.

This time I'm infuriated, "You asked me to sleep, so I turned off my light, now you want my light on?"

I want to kill this man, stop the bus and take the girl.

Soon the girl turns on her light and makes a phone call. The bus slows to a bridge crossing; this is where the girl will exit.

Her final words were, "It is too difficult for me to see you in the next city, come back in a month to my university."

Gone is the action erotic, a fantasy to be saved.

Trabzon Turkey. A mosque here, a church there, Russian women, Macdonald's along the Black Sea, I see them only at distance, my Georgian visa is my existence. On another bus I sit beside a nice man, he buys me a chi and then he buys me a piss, my money isn't good to him. A sexy Russian lady a seat in front turns, smiles, sends me words to share a taxi to the Georgian border. My answer is "Yes" and her response is, "We'll share costs onward to Batumi."

I'd been waiting for her to speak all day, some company, maybe some sex.

We cross the border, but she's taken in for questioning, I wait for one hour, that's all I can do, I'm on my way alone,

Georgia!

They say the water is cold; the Black Sea is warm to me.

Mother of Georgia, Christ and bells, Kazbegi beer, world famous mineral water sweet taste with power to heal. Television in Tbilisi seems a false unbelievable fable, happenings from ages ago or maybe future events, none of it real. I can't say what is history or future, real time has left me as I watch the screen in my room. Travel is as hard as love.

Unspeakable curiosity, I haven't a clue of where I'm going or what I'm doing. I'm addicted as Cassandra said. I never sleep, I jump from the planet so low and then I boil in the centre of the earth creating hatred and peace.

Awake the churches, hypnotize, such beauty ultimate attraction, architecture magnet attempts to seduce – Evil! And replace it with? Church is forbidden and I don't enter, I climb the hills to look at the view. What about Jesus? I haven't thought about Jesus only churches, they are the centre of architecture to lure. How can a man not fall to beauty? At the time it was churches and now it's corporate architecture. That's all. I travel the day and night thinking of Cassandra's hips up in the air and my body merging with hers.

"Is that how you see me?" Cassandra asks me as I couch in the lobby, approaching noon of her Istanbul hotel. My trip to Georgia done.

"From your belly button to your knees," I respond.

"Tell me more about the trip."

"What do you want me to tell? The coast has mountains and grand houses, black cars blocked streets with the help of men with guns, the USA commands from a large embassy. I don't know Georgia; people are friendly when they speak."

"You only know what you feel, and you felt television, religion, USA, expensive cars with guns, beer, food, and sea. That's all I asked and you said it well. I want more though. Length isn't important but I want more from you."

We walk up the street for refreshment and food. Outdoor café. Cassandra reads what I wrote again as we wait for coffee drinks.

"What about the girl, you've mildly described the scene, did you feel surrounded?"

"I loved the idea of walking off that bus with her and having an affair. I didn't feel surrounded, I felt restrained, unable to do as I please without a direct reason why. Only the obvious, the obvious I don't agree with. I wanted to hear the words, the reason why I was being hassled."

"The bus attendant never said anything to the girl to stop her from communicating with you?"

"I don't know what it was all about. I was born free."

"You were not born free – this is why you want to forget all you learned and start over for a time and then you will discover the same again."

I feel sullener than when I left Istanbul, a fog, an extreme sense of tiredness, frustration and disappointment.

Cassandra asks, "What's wrong?"

"I haven't found."

"I understand. Wait, you don't know what you'll find so you can only wait. At least you made it back on time. Give me your hand."

An icebreaker, Cassandra yawns and centres her face to mine while still holding my hand. "I met a man, an attractive charming boy. He sells carpets wouldn't you know."

"Did you buy a carpet?" I unleash her grip.

She continues, "Not yet . . . I suppose I will. I almost bought a carpet the last time I was here. I sort of promised him that when I came back, I would."

"So you haven't just met him?"

"Yes and no, I haven't slept with him, he hasn't made it into my room yet. I wished to take him away to the beach."

"You didn't?"

"No, I went alone. I promised myself the next time I saw him I'd spoil myself with him. So I want to take him away for a few days. Kidnap him seaside then dispose of him in Istanbul. A craving he is."

"Why didn't you take him away seaside? What stopped you?"

"Him, he's beautiful, lovely."

"That's not a reason."

"It's a reason because it would affect you and me."

"It won't conflict with us because your feelings for him aren't real."

"Correct. I'll have to break his heart. He can't break mine because he is only art, a mediocre carpet with a superb design."

"Is that fair if you're not serious?"

"To equal the unfairness of his extreme beauty."

With lunch, we make our way to the travel agency whereupon my ticket for Islamabad Pakistan is paid for; I will leave early the next morning.

Essay

———

A BREATH IS CAUGHT.

Fresh air with the news Cassandra is to spend time with another man.

Even my ticket is booted up to business class on Air Pakistan.

A fascinating Turkish man sits next to me and tells me it's okay to date a Turkish girl, "No problem."

It is his story of a magnificent Pakistan, "You can get anything in Pakistan – guns, girls, drugs. They'll deliver, I like Pakistan," that has me so intrigued I don't sleep on the 4:00 a.m. flight. I feel a shift in my esteem when I walk off the plane to Islamabad.

The people polite.

I wait at the airport all day.

I've purchased a flight to Peshawar. Night has fallen when I reach Peshawar.

I enter the street to another land, a thousand years ago, another planet, a million-dollar visit.

A man buys me a fruit drink, another feeds me rice and yet another man befriends me, he smiles his eyes glistening I can't refuse his offer, time stands still as we stare,

"Let's take a walk," he speaks.

I follow and we walk in the dark of Peshawar.

He's an enthusiastic apparition.

In minutes I've found a friend.

He questions. "I'm thirty years of age, how old are you?"

"Thirty-three."

We connect.

My feelings of life aren't suppressed. "What do you want to do?" he questions.

"Find a woman." Full of truth I speak, "I want to make love to a woman."

He is happy to hear such a claim, "I can't believe the way you speak. I've never heard a tourist say these words 'where can I find a woman'. You know, I've kissed a pussy in Russia. I want to kiss the pussy again," is his answer.

"You were in Russia?" happily I question.

"Yes, and I kiss a beautiful pussy, I fuck the pussy – I wish I had a camera to make a movie. Nobody here believes I kiss the pussy. I have to film it; they think I'm crazy here in Pakistan."

"I would do this for you if I had my camera with me."

"Where is your camera? I know a lady here in Peshawar, you can film me."

"My assistant has the camera."

"You have an assistant? Very good, you are an important man."

"I'm not important."

"But you have an assistant and you make films."

"Videos."

"Who is your assistant?" he questions.

"My assistant is a sweet angel."

"You sleep with her?" he asks intrigued.

"Yes, but we haven't had sex."

"What, you tell me you sleep with her and you don't have sex. She isn't pretty?"

"She's very attractive," I correct him.

"Yes she's pretty because you have a good face and you are a very strong man, you are a sportsman."

"I like sports."

"Yes I can tell by the way you walk, you are powerful. Most European's have a funny face, but your head is shaped well, you have a good face," flattering he is. "I want to kiss the pussy, make movies."

An old man in stupor stumbles near – brown sugar (heroin), his hand out for money. Meat cooked on a stick over coals dipped in sauce. We eat and talk in the dark alley drinking tea. All our dreams discussed.

I sleep long into the afternoon, penetrating noise, old city, the daylight has changed the scenery from strange moon of aliens to the bustling earth that I've seen photos of. I step into the street I'm famous, a man smiling and praying to my face when his hand reaches for change. A man asks me to give him a massage, I tell him to fuck off! Miniature fuel burns my eyes on the streets. Spinach is good.

Peshawar is a fantastic disaster I couldn't take another day.

What am I to write, what does she want me to say? Dust and dirt, a great mind-bending experience and now after four days I can't stand the noise and I haven't seen a woman. It's not true though; I saw some beautiful women today, I can't touch them or talk only stare and never dream because they are on higher ground, a ground so high I can't see. What do I write 'I go for a walk and many men smile'?

Cassandra has an experiment and I'm to work, my work is a documentary of my life.

And her experiment is?

I travel to the Northern Western Frontier Province. Like a heavy-duty acid trip, magic popping up everywhere, NWFP!

Disastrous mountain roads.

Kalasha Valley – Pagans.

My table at the top of the lawn, I'm a king. My glass of wine is filled, the hashish of the man is lit, the changing valley climate, the sound of the creek, the green and blue eyes of the children.

A man asks me to cross the mountain to Afghanistan. I promise to come back and stay for months.

If I was to describe Pakistan, I could go on forever. My eyes ears nose and mind have never been so alive. Through Swat Valley. Hunza Valley on the way to China. Karimabad – the hiking, the chatting, the tourists, the local's fascinating, sweet tea, Shangri la!

1930's dress. Lost in time again. I cross the Karakoram Pass thinking Jupiter, Mars, my binoculars on, "So this is earth?"

Kashgar, I'm in a donkey cart taxi. My first verse in Chinese.

In the evening I walk and find myself lost in the ancient where I've just come and the modern where I'll be. I haven't had an earth-shattering period only spurts, magnificent spurts, no ocean vessel, not lost at sea, Kashgar is the pinnacle of the trip near halfway. I buy a long black overcoat at the Sunday market looking like Mao. Kashgar is the perfect place to be, it's mixed up, the Muslim world and the Chinese world collide.

China – a picture to me, like the paintings in mist . . . other days I ask where is China? The loudest speakers blast propaganda, music, and a comedy team, the train stops when I don't want it to, and keeps moving when I expect it to stop. Chicken bones, peanut shells, piss, sunflower seeds, my socks never clean. I've fallen into a dream I love the train to Urumqi.

In Urumqi, I ask for a haircut and I'm offered a dreamy massage.

I catch a flight back to Islamabad and then on to Istanbul.

Cassandra is gone to Syria.

Damascus is landed in the late evening – a fruit drink stall before I sleep. I wake up to a set of beautiful wide eyes at the hotel's reception. I'm whisked to a bus station and go to meet Cassandra in Palmyra – the Bride of the Desert.

I've gone from the highest cold peaks to the warm desert, the middle of the silk trail to the start of the silk trail. My journey hasn't even begun and I could quit now today if I could have Cassandra for one day.

Palmyra. I walk the Ruins alone as Cassandra is not seen.

Evening comes and goes with little contact and by day Cassandra and I are sitting by a small swimming pool eating pomegranate when I pass her my notebook. She asks little as we tan – we retreat to the shade before she speaks.

"What? What was missing?" asks Cassandra.

"Contact, contact with women. After a few days in Peshawar, I was going crazy."

She goes on in silence reading before speaking, "The young man in Istanbul – I didn't sleep with him."

At first, I don't understand her, my intense interior world is dreaming something else.

"Why not?" cheerfully annoyed I announce.

"He didn't feel right, it wasn't important to sleep with him, just enjoy him and keep my rhythm up."

"And his," I remark with an underlying smile.

"Funny," she admits.

We arrive in Damascus quickly the next day and share a room with two women she'd met. I can roam Damascus alone as I like. The women of Damascus are beautiful. It is the most appealing city yet.

We all go out and see a movie. It is nice to have others around so our time together (Cassandra and I) isn't so weird; you could say we are relaxed. Work has taken a break, rest is sought.

Alone with Cassandra to the city of Maalula where Aramaic the language of Christ, is still spoken. The burning of the cross, singing songs loud, drinking alcohol, I want to be held. Our hands meet. My erection has begun with her again.

I can only hope her new friends vanish early in the morning so I can walk across the room and seduce her on the single bed.

We travel by car to Jordan with a couple of other passengers, a man and a woman who don't understand English.

Acting, improvising, killing time and divulging deep truths, exaggerated knowledge is the movie.

The camera rolls . . . I go first.

"The homes, the districts gone. My neighbours on the train gone. Motion, anticipation, fear, joy, we are common, we journey. I educate myself with travel. I study, read books amongst an ever-changing painting, an ever-evolving film."

Every word is my own natural purposeless truth.

"When did you start travelling?" I ask Cassandra.

Cassandra's words, her own on purpose.

"When I was a girl in school I travelled with my father and a little with my mother before my father died. By plane, boat, car, even bus but never by train, I desired train travel. I finished high school a half year early so I could work, save and travel without missing a beat. I attended university at age seventeen. An addiction followed, I found myself preferring to travel to destinations by train. I'd visit a city for two or three days, become bored and take the train. I never wanted to lose the high of a new place. The train is my relaxing state."

I'm beginning to understand I'm not attracted to her mind, not her eyes, and not her body, but her puzzle. Her oddity, a strange painting studied, viewed, and sought, with a different meaning every day.

"Is your addiction to new places or to travel?" I ask.

"Both, recline and atmosphere, the anticipation of place and the draw of escape."

"Are you finished schooling?"

It is her chance to speak of her life without being seduced.

"I don't know if I will ever be finished. My schooling has been paid for, for the rest of my life if I like. My travel money is my money, money I've made. I could travel each summer as a vacation from school, all arrangements taken care of by my family, but then it wouldn't be an addiction would it? Wealth is only freedom. I'd taken time off from school some time ago to travel. I worked the spring and summer to pay for the trip myself because travel for me is a fixation. If the money for travel was handed to me by my family no accomplishment or addiction just a trip, not life or death. I don't want a job. I don't want a career. I don't even want a degree. What I want is a passion. Why do you travel?" she asks.

My head is face down to answer humble. "Hide . . . travel isn't real, I'm not myself, travel isn't the planet I was raised."

"I travel because I don't want a place, I'm not hiding I'm not running I'm being."

"You don't want to settle down with a man?" calmly spoken by me.

"Maybe I'll travel the rails with a man alone and apart but together at the heart. I've never dated, I've only taken I haven't been taken. Men aren't at the centre of my life, though one man will be. Do you know your skin glistens? At times I can see through your skin, like as of right now."

She dives in my water, swims goodness, surfaces for air and takes my kind blood.

I intrude serenely, "You didn't have a boyfriend in university?"

She doesn't answer quickly.

Nothing matters . . . meditation is for others, we float on air traverse each other's bodies, we needn't food or water. Animals are nowhere near, nor humans. Hallucinations are others on the road in the cars we pass by, set pieces for me and her. We are heaven, Cassandra and I gods, the rest of the beings a film screen.

"I'm not a virgin," she finally answers, "I feed my desires but I don't fool myself, love hasn't come but once. And once will be enough. Aren't you looking for a woman to travel with?" Cassandra probes.

"No... I travel to find a woman and when found, I will stop and stay."

"You haven't friends?" she asks.

"Like you I suppose, I will be happy to see them and happy to leave them. No friends now – but maybe soon I will."

Cassandra motions for the man accompanying us to stop recording.

She leaves her character behind.

Cassandra speaks that my greatest weapon is my unique softness burned in intimidation. "You melt people and if they come very close, you burn with softness" is how she spoke it.

The car stops. Amman.

"I'm going to stay alone because we're getting too close, too close emotionally. There is more to learn than just about us."

Her words are emotional not staged. She adds, "What matters – death with you."

She walks away to the washroom smiling dizzy. I don't follow, I pace in the breeze. A hotel room sought, and a wonder of the world visited. The greatest wonder is each other.

At night in separate rooms, I harp on her soul with a black dagger.

I scribble in my notebook a passage I'll keep from Cassandra.

It is true, washing out every dream, my nights are filled eating through her panties but I stop myself, I never come.

I'll never masturbate again . . . only her.

Disillusion

———

AMMAN JORDAN, I'VE stopped writing.

She has a gallery of friends – resumed relations and new relations on the circuit. We reach Petra with her followers – frustration has set, sleep is faint – grouchy.

A cycle has begun; I can't sleep or want to sleep.

Cassandra does everything I don't want. I'm jealous.

We are eating, visiting sites, and returning for more humour with others, we are just living we are not advancing. Is this part of the movement? She tells others we are just travelling. She hasn't taken others to the centre of our existence, our movement. Has she forgotten? The trip is near done. What have we accomplished, scenery? New contacts for her address book? Even other women I may be interested in, she befriends with humour.

Wadi Rum, Lawrence of Arabia – sleep the desert two nights.

Aqaba. Feeling pale I've made plans to go ahead to Jerusalem without Cassandra. She accepts this.

Something has changed in Aqaba. Swimming is needed.

After my swim – I wander the streets, heat and dust again. A centre street, Cassandra chats with her gallery.

Before I engage the gathering of friends, Cassandra advances towards me.

She brushes by me.

Her breasts deliberate against my shirt, against my chest.

Her eyes straight at mine her voice soft, "Sleep in my room this afternoon."

I pause – before I turn and follow. She doesn't say goodbye to her gathering of friends.

"I have a nice room." She says as I swallow.

Her key is fetched, our hands clasp. We proceed to the staircase to the hall and to her room.

"Here is a towel," she walks towards the bathroom.

I drop my clothing. Put the towel on.

"Shower?" she asks.

"No," I answer.

"Very hot – do you want to turn the fan on?"

"No," I answer.

"Wait." She speaks while in the bathroom.

She walks out of the bathroom in a thin towel.

Her towel falls, her body exposed, savoured.

Free no condom.

My entire body is now cock, every muscle she touches feels head.

Her body splits in half and surrounds me internally.

Vulnerable strokes skin on skin.

I lift her to the floor to stop my volcano from an abrupt end.

Smashing delight her ear to the floor, her eye to the crack of the door.

Hold still.

Catch some breath. It is over.

She dresses.

"I'll get some food for me and you."

With my smell still with her, she walks out the door.

I don't want to move – the heat, the sweat, I must move to shower.

In the real world, we would have started to fuck that instant that moment when she came against me on the dusty road.

With her few words in a flash, I discover that she'll be a dependency. It isn't talk, it is never talk, you don't have to say a word to the one you truly want. Harmony is there and peace already. Talk is only manipulative. She is wicked in her mind. She never misses a beat cramming time to make more time.

Old and young beware of her, the young blinded, and the old intrigued. She hasn't even had a chance to date and not a need, she only looks for a special one. She couldn't wait to be an adult to get on with her life. She can make love to a woman mentally as well as she can to a man physically, though if you're not in her domain she just seems strange. She will have all of you or none of you. The camera, recordings, and videos of her unique life to be studied, she lives as a movie. Each season her aims are the same – discovery, knowledge, and advancement. Her depth far reaches any conversation that may be held with her. Strum, strum, strum, hypnotized, she is above the universe it is all a laugh, a game. Always one on one, many is not important, only one at a time she teaches and learns. She is remote, not of the age she lives and without the necessary capabilities to make change. A brilliant idiot, she is.

The notebook is set down.

"Is this me?" Cassandra comments with laughter after reading what I've just wrote. Now back in the room after retrieving food for us.

"Is it?" I answer in question.

"This is all you've wrote?"

"I've just wrote this. I haven't written anything else. I'm not supposed to give an account of place to place, scene to scene, I met fellow travellers – some gave me a headache, others interest."

"And what about me, you say I'm a dependency, elaborate."

"I say you're becoming a dependency . . . family."

"Like a sister?"

"More."

"A wife!" she screams.

"I said becoming . . . you're becoming a dependency you haven't evolved to that dependent state yet."

"You build steps, you want nothing for free. A beautiful woman you won't take until you deserve."

"Clever," I surmise.

"I'm speaking for you."

"I can't say why you've let me into your bed, only you can."

"Tell me, has the experiment been a success?"

"A success for me, all my emotions still here but I ignore them, numb to my past."

"So you have emotions of the past?"

"Yes," I answer.

"Nothing has changed you still have to go to Jerusalem without me. We will meet in Tel Aviv. Find your own way and when you are finished, we will be as one. Fiction first and soon it will become as real as our movement."

"What is our movement?" I ask.

"It hasn't happened. As all, it will be in the future."

"I'll ask you again Cassandra – what is our movement?"

"What we think, others will think. I don't have the answers."

"What do we think Cassandra?"

"We know more than what we've been told. We don't have to speak we must only create in our internal and this will change to the external."

"What are we creating?" I ask.

"I don't know. You know. It is you who asked the questions to your own answers. You better go stay in your hotel tonight – I would like to be alone. Go to Jerusalem without me. If you go with me, you will only have thoughts of me."

Now my thoughts will be when will we fuck again?

"I will see you soon in Tel Aviv, bring me something good," she requests.

I haven't had Cassandra for a day, only a couple of hours. Any other man she'd chew, suck his juices and spit away, conquering lust. For herself, for me, she'll suffer.

I set off for Jerusalem.

A horror in cat piss – forty backpackers on a rooftop with ten cats – like a refugee camp I stay. I've done what she trained, follow a gallery of travellers.

I was sick at the Dead Sea – and got sicker every day.

Jerusalem is the place where God lovers want to stay.

Salvation – your divine – the Wailing Wall I near cried in the fine evening light.

Dome of the Rock; walked there too.

The crucifix also passed on the next street.

Am I the only one who can't feel?

I can't stay. Sorry, Cassandra maybe I miss you.

Jerusalem, I have found un-comfort.

I think Cassandra with an added notion that ancient religion must be forgotten and modern ideology must be neglected to solve the puzzle of being.

The answer is clear . . . why look for a God outside when we can find our own inside.

The simplest form to follow is your inside.

All that was ever on the outside is also the inside and so on.

This will have to be enough for her.

Discotheque

TEL AVIV

Hello Cassandra.

I've left Jerusalem after only a few days.

I don't have to wait for her – she's waiting for me in Tel Aviv.

Cassandra passes me the key to her plush room. I fall asleep alone. I can't touch myself . . . so close to explode when Cassandra enters the room.

"Getting some rest?"

"Yes."

"Good – I'll take a shower we're going dancing. We haven't danced. Put on your best suit."

A long walk, eat, walk, drink, walk, drink, and then . . . Electricity! I have arrived in 2000, clothing, sounds, my eyes, my mind bulging. Dancing. Even Cassandra is lost from my thoughts in the atmosphere of Discotheque. Strangeness accumulates, alcohol affects drift because we are dancing. By the late evening, I can't tell if the beautiful woman across the dance floor is a boy or a girl. Cassandra I've lost track of her – she stares from behind a railing and walks away disappears. In time I notice she is truly gone. I stumble out; ramble to find her hotel room.

I enter her room.

Cassandra in trance gives ear sleeping restlessly. My eyes speed on her lingerie.

Her finger flirts with the red strap above her breast.

I open the covers and lay to bed.

My hand grasps her hand. I roll to my stomach placing my warmth to her flat grip.

Cassandra speaks, "You can put some music on, play that soft one, Radio Head."

I open the computer and select the song.

When I turn back, she seems asleep. I hesitate. She rolls to my side her leg is instant on mine.

I'm boundless in energy.

The buzzes of the earth's electrical wires that burn my brain are gone.

Naked . . . hydrofoil above the bed, yoga manoeuvres sprung in desires to taste each other.

The room is cool.

Blur – and time, we sleep.

We wake still clutching – fucking.

A conversation – I'm glad we ate.

"Have you been with any other women?" she asks.

Can I tell her all my truths?

She tells, "Go deep – I told you this before, surface conversation destroys my craving for you."

"Sometimes I thought to seduce other women in Syria and Jordan, but you interceded." With whom? She must wonder. "No one in particular, no woman stole my heart for a day. The locals I wanted dearly."

"Didn't they have women at The Retreat?"

"Many," I claim.

"Nothing happened when you were in retreat?"

"Thoughts."

"About who?" Cassandra, cool.

"All of them – I had assistants."

"Anyone else? What about the Designer – I heard she kissed you."

"How did you hear that?"

"It is my job to know what you were up to. I know almost every move you made."

"What else do you know?"

"Your ex-girlfriend came to see you."

"I want to know everything – has The Retreat infiltrated me?"

"What does that mean?" She sits up, "You think that we have travelled inside your head and controlled your thoughts?" She pouts. "You have used us. We did not create you, you created us. I can see how your ex-girlfriend feels. I used to hate her, now I understand her; you create a world you dream. It isn't real for you, only a dream and when you wake you say goodbye that was fun but not real. What is real for you?"

"You know the answer, Cassandra. My internal is real."

"Yes, but I must live in the external with you."

"You've created me."

"And you've created my world."

"Our world, I sometimes think my world is all your design," is my thought out loud.

"All yours," hot air released by her. "I suggested you to Karen and the rest was you and her, I didn't have input, I trusted you. My only influence was Nadia."

"So Nadia has been a part of this from the beginning?"

"You look disappointed."

Only silence.

Cassandra breaks the silence. "I know you went to her place. Nadia was a great friend of mine, she may still be, but as her success accumulates, I'll become more of a strength overcome than a weakness sought. She liked you very much. In general, she knew all about you. I told her of you and of us in Europe, you were an ongoing gossip story. She even came over to The Retreat and spied on you. We sent messages to you. We even masturbated. I'd imagine tasting her and then I'd cry. We sent soft sounds of lust through the speakers while you slept. We picked music for you, designed all your clothing, that's how your clothing was done so fast – pre-made. Your brain listened to us as you waited in retreat. She'd already decided what you'd be wearing and you fell right into her conception of fashion."

"What else did I fall into?"

Programmed, follow.

I'm not amazed they've put thoughts in my brain. Have I put the words I've heard in their mouths? I wonder. An unidentifiable source, a nonexistent place of discussion, no rules, this is our movement. Take away conspiracy theory. Don't dwell on paranoid delusions of being controlled. A movement thought simultaneously and moved by fabric and thread. An accumulation of brain waves hardened cast. Our path already seen in each other's concealed mind. Thoughts gather if mixed in good taste the thoughts move to an earthly realm.

"Our movement has no reference it isn't a faith, but a performance improvised after practised in each of our minds."

"Internal is more than mind it is the beats of time," I add.

"Always the truth unless you must lie to find truth," she adds.

"Connect lies until you have truth."

"Nadia was supposed to be a virgin – was she?"

"No," I answer.

"You are both liars – she isn't a virgin and you made love to her."

"So?"

"So – she crossed me."

"How did she cross you?"

"By kissing you at The Retreat. You were to kiss her if you wanted. She wasn't to seduce you first."

"Sorry I didn't read the rules."

"Who else did you break the rules with?"

"I've thought about breaking the rules with Karen."

"What, you think you could fuck Karen – my mother?"

"What – what did you say?" I exclaim.

"How long was it going to take you? Karen is my mom."

"Karen is your mom?"

"You've gone too far – do you love Nadia?"

I can't speak.

She speaks. "Forget it."

A tear begins to stream. Hands to her face, eyes blaring hurt, to the bathroom she crumples.

Still . . . I haven't shock, anger, or embarrassment. I'm smiling. The television volume is down. I turn off the television and straighten out the room.

Cassandra returns, "Did you fuck anyone else?"

"I didn't want to hurt you."

"Write I fucked my lover's best friend and want to fuck her again and now I want to fuck my lover's mother."

"Since when have we been lovers?"

"We've been lovers internally since we met – don't deny it. Are you sorry that you didn't know she was my mother or that you've talked about someone I have a connection to? It doesn't even matter if she's my mother, you know that I know Karen, she is not a part of our fiction, she is in our lives. You don't understand, can't you figure it out. You made love to Nadia my friend. Every other woman on this trip I couldn't care – even if you had sex with the assistants I wouldn't care, they were objects placed for you. You were mine. I have to go."

In the morning everything is wrong.

Cassandra left a note and an air ticket.

The note read: "You have done nothing wrong you just don't understand me. The hotel room has been paid until you fly out.

Someone will pick you up at the airport in Vancouver and your contract will be fulfilled".

I understand her it is true she has been my lover internally, in my heart, in my future since we met. Love unseen, love on the inside. We both knew it would happen on the outside because we were lovers internally.

All that I've worked for is still only sex and debate momentarily – unsettled.

Can we find passion in a motionless setting?

Will stagnation kill us or will we continue to kill each other from a distance?

All that I'd wished happened, yet I still hold back.

I want unadulterated sex.

I don't know how the human face smiles. No falsified thoughts groomed to compel the person to read. I'm no longer the poet thinking of words for Cassandra.

The androgynous-looking assistant is what I think on the flight to Vancouver, her body translucent, odd, sexy.

Frank

———

THE SEASON HAS FINISHED . . . back to basics, swiss cheese, deliberate hallucinations, the gifts haven't been forgotten, renewed psychosis acknowledged. Accept a mission so implausible but possible. I'm crazy in strong capitals, I like crazy, nothing is real. Earth is a joke, a playground for serious beings, examples of life . . . we always wait to sit until we stand.

There is Karen, waiting in arrivals. Will Karen accept me as the monkey returned? Her enthusiasm is tremendous, her hug stupendous, a schoolyard girl giggling.

At The Retreat, everyone is missing.

"Where is everyone, on vacation?" I ask.

"No, everything is normal."

"What happened to my assistants?"

"You said it, your assistants; their services aren't required since you are no longer here."

"And the doctor?"

"Paul is off for a few days. He asked for you to call him – here is his number."

"I can't believe it."

"All the work you've done will be passed on to us by Cassandra – you have fulfilled your contract. If you want to leave you can, or you can continue on with Cassandra. She will be back in a few days."

"She will see me?"

"What do you think?"

"I don't think."

Everything is discussed with Karen on my personal finances – my home and my truck sold. Pay from The Retreat to be deposited in my account.

I have more money than I have ever had – and yet I have less material than I've ever had. All personal items have also been auctioned off. I have what Nadia designed or bought, that is all.

Karen says, "We have done our part, you can see now we haven't hurt you. Please, you can give us a good review. Would you pay for your time here if you knew what you know now?"

"Yes."

"All the material on you isn't to harm you."

"You and Cassandra..." I've stopped in mid-sentence.

"When you have children, you will understand."

I don't stay at The Retreat; it has no use – no one to see – Karen takes me to a hotel and I check in.

Extreme rest is the subject. Lonely, I haven't a home my strength is left behind in travels.

I walk down the street where I'd made love to Nadia the designer.

I don't know if I'll enter her store, I must pass by. If Nadia is near the window or alone if eye contact is made I'll stop and enter.

Nothing, paper covers the windows and "For lease" is spelled on the door, no forward address.

I'm silly imagining Nadia passing on the street.

I call Paul Louis.

He will see me the next day immediately.

We met for dinner.

"Hello Doctor, how are you?"

"Paul Louis is fine – don't call me 'Doctor.'"

"What? Why?" I ask.

"I was never a doctor and likely will never be – I'm a medic."

"Why do they call you Doctor?"

"They don't, you do, and I never stopped you. Karen never stopped you, if you asked you would have been told the truth, but you didn't ask. You just assumed because I checked your blood pressure and my clothing is similar to that of a doctor.

I hold a supervisory position at The Retreat. I started as temporary and progressed to a private hire by her. A good relationship with Karen developed along with some good ideas. I'm not all that comfortable taking care of car wrecks and The Retreat is a nice alternative. The best pay, interesting work, a position, a label."

"A small office."

"Yes – a small office."

"Do you know Karen's daughter?"

"We are acquainted – I've kept my distance over the years and Karen has us at a distance. I know you went travelling with her. I wasn't privileged to all that was happening with you after your time at The Retreat, or before when you met Cassandra. Details weren't given except you'd be going with Cassandra on an extension of your time at The Retreat. That's all. Cassandra doesn't spend a lot of time with staff at The Retreat. We have short polite conversations. I don't work directly with her. I work with Karen and others you haven't met. You are a different project."

"So you aren't involved with my show?"

"Not in the specific, I see that you are healthy. I give you the help you need, and if I can't solve the problem, I find you someone who can. When your experiment is documented, I will know, like everyone else."

"What about Nadia – the designer?"

"Same. Can't miss her, a beautiful woman, she made my uniform and your clothing. You have done this yourself, everything you created is just like you said the first day you walked into The Retreat. I laughed when I first talked to you and told Karen to ignore you but she wouldn't. At the time I didn't know you were in deep with Cassandra."

I answer him directly. "I made a suggestion, a trigger word, Cassandra and Karen set everything on the table. I just walked in."

"And now?" he asks.

"My short journey in China has given me an interest in the East. Something new – go somewhere?"

"Let me know – I'm looking to do something away from The Retreat."

"Any ideas?"

"Cambodia," he suggests.

Paul Louis the medic will be my friend.

Very early in the morning a call to my room.

Cassandra is in the Lobby and comes up to my room.

Jet lag keeps me awake at 3:30 am.

She is jet lagged too. Harmless, alone, and complete, no sketching, no note-taking, no camera, no novel or baggage only the protection of her clothing. She isn't as tall as she once seemed and prettier than I remember, less fierce.

Fearless she stands.

"Can I fall asleep here?" she asks.

"Yes."

Time together.

"Your mother is different from you. You look alike." I comment.

"We look alike? If we look alike, how come you couldn't tell?"

"Different traits," I state.

"Like what?"

"I don't know, just different."

"We're the same."

"Why don't you call her Mom?"

"Work – it doesn't sound professional besides I pretend she isn't my mother."

"If you'd called her Mom, I'd been able to guess that Karen was your mother and been a lot less confused."

"I'm different than my father, he was kind. I didn't have to understand him or try to. I felt no crime or pressure of him. He was like a man should be. He didn't confuse me."

"Your mother has?"

"Call her Karen. Karen comes and goes with smiles and a whip."

"That is her, exactly."

"I've been studying her since I was twelve. Before that, she was only beauty. My father died when I was thirteen. We travelled tight, me and my father for one year. He lived for me and ruled with a sword exactly the opposite of the way he commanded his wife. He was sick for the last month we travelled. The last year he lived, I stayed with my mother. Dad didn't want me to see him dissolve to death. My mom had known for two years he was to die. I'm sure she counted the days to freedom, but when he died there wasn't celebration. She loved him, but she couldn't face taking care of him. Mother already had her future in place. My father never had more than two drinks in a night his entire life. He wasn't a ladies' man, women I'm sure petrified him. He married my mother because she asked him. He was that kind of man. He was everything she wasn't with enough money to seduce a beautiful girl. She killed him."

"How?" is shuttled quickly from my mouth.

"She killed him with kindness. She was more than he'd asked for. She became more powerful, more important than him, she overwhelmed him. She didn't need him. Once she was in motion, her own movement capsized his. She worked, increased her wealth. When I began university, she began the idea of the Spa/Retreat. My father married early but his first wife found him boring and left him. You know what Karen's job was when she met my father?"

"No."

"A stewardess. They met high in the sky, slow and mutual, she was pregnant fast, that's how they did it. Still love her?"

"Yes, I suppose."

"When all the papers are flipped, she's just a person the veneer can be applied to anyone. I didn't know Karen's clout until I stayed with her before my father died. She answered questions and gave orders from morning till night, always charming never losing her cool, I was mesmerized, and she managed to fit me into everything. When Father died, Mother and Cassandra ended, and we became Karen and K, family shit was dead, we hung out; we didn't take or give orders."

Soon we fall asleep, we don't make love.

Cassandra wakes and goes into speech, "India or Africa when you are ready. The Taj Mahal with the one I love. If you're not the one, don't come. All day I work and exercise. At night I'm starved to explore, will I explore the nights with or without you? An invitation is what I have suggested. Africa or India?"

"For work or play?"

"Both, except you won't be getting paid. We can finish the book we are writing. Bring our work together."

I haven't a fast answer for her. "Yes, but I need several months alone."

"To find what?" she's direct.

"I'm going to live in Cambodia."

"And what about me?" she questions.

"Nothing, wait," I answer her.

"You're doing it again?"

"Doing what?" I ask.

"I haven't fear, and I haven't hate. I want to do as you and run from the pulse that beats down my brain to burst in my heart. Unlike you, I will stay and conquer cruel demons swimming in my veins."

She hasn't dry eyes, no she isn't crying or tearing nor evidence, but she hasn't dry eyes.

"You want to find Nadia?" she asks.

"I don't know."

"Nadia's gone to England – she's opening a shop – she's married. You still want to find her?"

"Sometimes."

"Go to England – she said she'd fuck you if she saw you."

"Is that really what she said?"

"Yeah, I told her nothing happened between us, you're all hers."

"What about her husband?"

"Nothing – she'll keep you close until her husband finds out, and then she'll make a decision."

"Stop," I plead.

"London, England." She almost screams.

She speaks softly after time, "I blame the experiment . . . we are casualties of something bigger than our togetherness. Our movement will continue."

I argue, "What movement? What followers do we have, what is our agenda?"

"Please. Go watch the men in South East Asia play. What I have done is no different – you've benefited and I've invested. I'm in love but I always knew I'd walk away before you'd break my heart. When someone buys something, they treat it as their own, they don't like another to touch their stuff like Nadia did. She stole you."

"Why the elaborate story?" I ask.

"I gave you what you dreamt, so be happy. You wanted a new world new age philosophy, and now you have it. You were easy – The Retreat is just a spa that you stayed for too long, and my mom paid. That was it, you were just a man I wanted to have. I'm a modern woman and don't tell me men don't go to the same lengths to procure a woman. Hell, you only had to wait seven months – besides I was too busy for you during this time. Six months because that's all the mind can stand to wait. But I gave you seven months because I wanted you slightly deranged. I even sent you to travel alone, so I could pursue others. I knew you wouldn't find another woman, all those pretty assistants you had at The Retreat and you didn't come close to touching them, except Nadia, and you wouldn't have touched her either if she hadn't seduced you. I suppose there was the chance of another woman seducing you but I kept you on a tight schedule."

Cassandra is consistent – she walks out on me.

Everything she says I can say I put to her mind. She's got her wish and I got mine. A movement of two, our inside justified, the outside world cruel. We constitute the world from within. All occurs behind the scenes, what is seen is not to be believed. Battling outside influence is our purpose. Our pleasure is taking the mind inward to its limits, and our defeat is accepting faint, and our responsibility is the gift of what we hold inside. We must read the placing and positions of others because essentially, we have placed the objects, persons, and speech for unknown reasons. This is what we think simultaneously.

Placid

———

PAUL LOUIS HAS BEEN waiting patiently for my plans – we have been in steady contact.

We've met at the same lounge as we did the night before I left on my adventure with Cassandra.

"I'm going to Cambodia," I tell him.

"Take me with you." He answers quickly.

"What about work?"

"Quit." He smiles.

"You're not going to quit, it is the best job, you said it yourself."

"True – I'll ask Karen for a leave of absence, a one-year leave. She'll say yes because I'm going with you. Maybe she'll pay us." He laughs.

"It must be a family thing," I add.

"To own who they fuck?"

"Or is it us, Paul? Have we seduced this mother and daughter to get what we must? You aren't really in love with Karen, are you?"

"No – I suspect not, this happens at work, feelings develop and other relationships are destroyed."

"And now we are a team, Paul."

"Let's go find a mother and daughter, this time you will have to take the mother."

"We won't find it here – unless your cocktail girl has a very attractive young mother."

"My cocktail girl no longer works here – I don't see her anymore."

"What happened?" I ask.

"She stopped working and I stopped calling." He answers.

"There was another cocktail girl that worked here – a ripe dignified nymph? She served me last time."

"Yes, I remember. Are you now interested? I have her number – but there is something I must tell you."

"What?"

"I paid her to pay attention to you. She would have spent the night with you for a price."

"That was nice of you."

"I thought so. I did pay her a very nice sum to spark your interest. "

"But unsuccessful, if she was here tonight...."

"If she was here tonight my investment would have been well spent, is what you are saying."

He is correct.

I change the subject.

"You know I contacted my ex-girlfriend yesterday."

"Your girlfriend before you did the experiment at The Retreat?"

"Yes, my former girlfriend, you remember she came to The Retreat."

"Why did you contact her?" he asks.

"To see what happened to her – what she thought."

"What did she think?" he asks.

"I called and she said, 'Did you have a good time on your trip fucking around the world?' I answered, 'What do you mean?' And she said, 'You just wanted to go fuck a girl in every other country you could – so were they better than me?' I answered, 'Different'. In the end, she said she'd met someone else when I was in retreat but has since dissolved the relationship. After her initial assault, she was really nice and would like to come to Cambodia for a visit – she still talks to my mom every so often."

"Will you see her?"

"It's all just friendly talk."

"That is all you needed – friendly talk."

"And your wife?" I ask Paul.

"Nothing – wife isn't the same as ex-girlfriend, we are still separated."

The night ended early with our plan to travel to Cambodia intact.

I'll stay with my sister's family in Vancouver for now. After neglecting my parents I'll return to their door too.

Placid – I don't want any responsibility.

Does Cassandra do the same today – patching our story together in her own platform for someone to see? A man programmed to carry her thoughts to the world, is this what Cassandra writes? Until this time I'd reasoned it was Karen – Karen the mastermind of The Retreat for Cassandra, a place for Cassandra in a society that hasn't a place for a strange girl as she. I hadn't thought deep enough until this day, I hadn't thought of the movement. The movement travels invisibly. Amazing to think Karen has accomplished this for Cassandra alone. It is Cassandra who has created this world. Cassandra has empowered her mother, though Cassandra resists belief in her own powers. There is no confusion. Karen and Cassandra rule their universe. The result is a movement among people for a common goal. No words, only dreams that consolidate to life. Unknowingly together, Cassandra thought the creation of The Retreat and Karen provided.

The Retreat took care of me perfectly – I always had money, food, shelter, not to mention motion.

Now I will do the same.

Environment

―――

CAMBODIA

I live in a neighbourhood in Pursat province.

I've purchased a one-room house.

A lot of dancing and drinking – at first it is was fun but soon just noise and clever lies to disguise my dislike of mind-numbing alcohol. The dancing and singing are enjoyed when at a viable volume.

God is still around – there is a mosque in my community, a church in the next community. For the most part, I deal with superstition, rituals, myths and spirits more so than Buddha's teachings.

My neighbour told me I couldn't plant a certain kind of tree on my land. "Bad spirit's," she said. The yard I want isn't easy.

My neighbour's daughter has been visiting daily – she started coming over when I mentioned I had a problem with rats running along the rafters disturbing my sleep. She claimed to be number one rat killer. I asked her to come over and set a trap or do whatever she does to kill.

She scolded me "Cambodians cannot kill rats – you foreigner will kill."

Stunned I was about to say "sorry" when she started to laugh and spoke, "Tonight I kill rat for you."

And that is how it started, my schooling – except she doesn't help me learn Cambodian – she's stern, "I don't want you speaking to anyone else – or learning too much."

I have little money to spend. I have a computer and two batteries that are charged daily down the street. My house is next to several empty lots and behind these empty lots is a paved road next to the river bank. I'd wade in the river daily – until I bought a dugout canoe. Now I do more than wade – though slowly there is less and less water.

I think to eat at home though once a day I eat out – a daily choice between three restaurants. I go to the market almost every day. The market is where I learn the most. Lately, I haven't travelled to the market, my neighbour's daughter does this for me – I think she's twenty-three.

My house is middle of the road compared to most, bad but not the worst on the dirt road I live. The lease ownership of my house was negotiated by my fixer.

When one comes to a new country he finds a friend, an interpreter, an entrepreneur, a fixer. Fixer is a real estate agent without a license. He is a driver – a communicator, he handles logistics. Fixer is a friend who benefits financially from the friendship, I benefit from his knowledge, skills and protection.

Fixer works with Paul Louis daily. Paul is in charge of dispensing the money. I pretend none of the money existed.

I received a fair amount of money from The Retreat, though less than I made from the sale of my home, truck, and other possessions. We discussed much of what we should do with the money. It was thought a sports complex – a place for kids to learn sports and then it was thought a park for families and the elderly to go. Sure we thought about the poor, give food. I almost switched all my thoughts to the arts – but it was to Paul Louis's strength that I went.

We started a team – a nurse, a medic, a dental assistant, and Fixer.

There was the question of how much money I would give – after much consultation with Paul Louis I decided to give all of my money away, except for five thousand that will stay in a safety deposit box in Canada. A practical allowance is also set aside to take care of my daily needs for the year. I decided to buy transportation in Cambodia. A four-door Toyota truck is bought with a high canopy for the team to use, and a Honda 125 motto for my own transportation.

Paul was afraid we wouldn't be able to survive for six months let alone one year. I wasn't worried, "I'll live on nothing," I said.

The team travels in the truck serving the needy with medical and dental consultation educating hygiene and offering necessities. I can't answer all the services they do – I haven't seen them.

When busy I don't think or need anything just peace – but when I'm not busy I think about having fun and improving my yard, planting, digging, building a stone patio. Maybe I can put new wooden flooring down. I have a propane stove, a double burner.

Romantic simple is the best.

At first, it was simple, I wanted nothing – now with improvements my yard is becoming the best on the block.

It is a problem when I know I have five thousand dollars in a safety deposit box in Canada. Fuck I'm supposed to have nothing – live in the middle of a village in a tent. My neighbours just assume that I need electricity – a new toilet. Power has come – it is a rescue from the heat, though I spent $30 for a fan. A monthly power bill too. This isn't my only convenience. I've started to travel to Phnom Penh the Capital city regularly.

I tried to contact Paul Louis the other day – his phone was closed. I use this as an excuse to travel to Phnom Penh an anything can happen place of day and night. This is where the charity has an office combined house where Paul Louis and others stay when in the city.

Paul isn't to be found.

Fixer is sought and found. "I don't want to tell you," Fixer says. "Paul is in Vietnam. He's left with his girlfriend. He has a girlfriend now."

I reach the dental assistant; she is scared Paul will spend the money we need to do our work. "He's been buying his girlfriend gold jewellery," she spoke.

I decide not to stay at the office house. I don't want to surprise Paul, shock him that I'm here, so I drift to the ocean for a couple of days depleting my budget.

I return to Phnom Penh and try to expel deceit and disappointment from my thoughts. Paul Louis just isn't a crooked kind of man.

Paul is waiting for me.

"You've been busy with your girlfriend?" I'm blunt.

"Very busy," he answers.

No lies here.

He adds, "Even charities need a break."

"They do," I answer.

"I imagine you have heard stories – and they are all true. Don't worry, all your money is intact – I've been using my own money. All your dreams are safe."

"And yours?" I confront Paul.

"If I spent all my money it wouldn't matter. I like her – she makes my stay nice. I haven't bothered to tell you about her – I wanted to, and maybe I've been wrong not to tell you I'd left for Vietnam. You know about these things with women – a person has to keep things secret for a time if they are to work out."

"That's why they call it personal relationships," I answer him.

Paul goes on, "I have become entranced with her – she doesn't know the earth is round or that the world is covered by ocean. It isn't that she doesn't know she doesn't care to believe. Her thoughts are like you, internal, there isn't place, it is all here. So remarkable she says Khmer people aren't supposed to go anywhere, everything they need is here."

"You sound like I used to."

"Yes, when I first met you, you talked like her." Paul Louis goes on. "At first I laughed at her, now I understand her perception of what the world and universe are – she sees something we don't, the common scientific perception is only the shelter of something we can't imagine."

I look at his expression, his happiness, he's found what he'd looked for.

"You have been struck by lightning," I answer him.

"Yes, and I've spent less than what I spent on the cocktail girl back home. Though this woman makes my head spin."

"I understand Paul. I too have a woman speaking things I have never heard, never thought. And I don't know what to do about her."

"Who is she?"

"My neighbours' daughter – she has charmed my heart"

"So what will you do?"

"Move."

He laughs very hard.

"What about our work?" I ask.

"We can do an evaluation soon. What do you think? Things are as expected, my crew will continue to do our work and your community garden will grow – as for money, you are below budget."

"How long can we last?"

"Forever," he laughs.

"You can go back to Pursat and relax – finish your book."

"Do I have to go back? I'd rather enjoy myself here."

"You've tired of your house?"

"I like where I stay. I also like coming here, you know watch TV, go out dancing. I miss things, Paul. I wish I could watch the ice hockey playoffs."

"What has happened to you?" he asks.

"The environment."

Paul shakes his head. "There isn't anything easy. Nothing is easy here – it is all a myth. There is no more solitude in the world. We are all material beings of the first world. We are lucky we've come here now before the ATMs and the rest of the West. Keep writing like you've been doing and in time you will find that everything is fine, you haven't missed anything. I promise you – time is only a watch."

I listened to Paul Louis and returned immediately to my home, forsaking the nightlife of Phnom Penh. I have been swayed by wants and what I think I should believe. Paul's words have changed me to where I'd liked to be – no more thoughts of advancing, consuming, just live within my means – finish what I'd intended to finish.

My lifestyle, my answers have come too late. My money is about to run out. I can see it finished in weeks not months. I've retreated shy of my neighbours with the little money I have to give and spend. Can foreigner set up a stand and sell? This is what I should do, this is what a man has to do – but I can't – too much wealth where I come from. I won't be able to manage until the end of my time.

I've finished writing my book.

I can hear a vehicle at the gate of my yard.

Paul Louis and Fixer are here.

"More than halfway done." Paul can be heard.

"I can't stay for the rain," I answer.

Fixer and Paul laugh, they know my truth. "Don't stop, come in business with us. We have set up everything it isn't much but you can continue on writing – except we will travel the country – you want to sell your house?"

"Ha-maybe," this makes me laugh.

Paul knew somehow – all an adventure with an escape hatch.

"You can't live as you have and then go back to the start; this is very hard to do – I couldn't see you suffer. All your money is in a bank account, except the money that the Spa/Retreat gave you, it was invested getting the charity and business going. We are close to making a profit. You didn't say anything about non-profit, so we have profited from the rich and given to the poor. It is the criminals' trick; we aren't criminals though because we didn't steal the money. We charged for services. You have a nice half hectare of land to do what you want on the coast. A bank account full of the money – so what will you do, run away to India, England, or stay here and start what you thought you had finished?"

"You are rich," Fixer says to me.

"Where do we start?" I ask.

"Pack up and come with us."

"What about my house here?" I question, still not understanding if they speak the truth.

"Give your neighbour a few dollars to watch the place. After a tour, you can come back – sell the place – or even better give it to your neighbour's daughter."

"Yes – I'll give her the land and house. What about your woman – will you marry, buy land?" I ask Paul.

"I won't marry – I can't marry, I'm married."

"Where did you get the money, tell me the truth – was it Karen?" I ask.

"No not Karen, Karen's contacts. We've made our own money or at least the money that we need to eat and live with. We give to the poor and charge the rich it is two companies we have – it was Fixer's idea. You can join us and have food and shelter to survive your daily needs as we do. I don't know what job you will do. I think we can't afford you, but it is your truck your charity – our company. We are all happy, but we'd like a bigger team – join us."

There was a time when Cambodia didn't have money. What would life be like if every family had a plot of land?

Fixer and Paul Louis smile wide. They don't know how to solve either.

I think there was a time when people devoted their life's to something and I think that time has passed – we can devote for a time, forget and carry on to a new devotion – the time of life with one religion – one of anything is maybe something that could be done if life was ordinary – but life is unique.

⚓

End

Travel experiences of the late 90s early 2000s became a novel. Of course, the reality was more exciting than the book. You must keep some things for yourself. Les Cook

Read a sample of – *Lit for Nothin*

by Les Cook

—

End this perfect life now so I can begin.

She looked at me and said, 'You are that used to death, that you can say it so calm like that?'

I'm not used to death – I'm used to hearing it . . . that is all.

I made a decision eighteen months ago, as I stood at my open bedroom door looking past my wife to the empty hall – it wasn't a specific thing I was going to change; it was going to be a sale.

A tunnel of hell blew through my mind soul universe – the sound barrier burst my ears to a slight non-painful tinge as I travelled near the speed of light until quiet, alone, dark, and hollow.

No longer travelling forwards or backwards.

When you travel this fast, you stop moving, find harmony.

I knew it would be more than a few months of heartache to reach peace.

'Hell' some would say.... I don't believe in 'Hell' – I'll come out the other-side.

Cell of horror – let us be real, it is minor compared to what some feel – this is education, not competition.

The deal made the decision conceived is mine alone – one man, one secret – can't tell a soul otherwise someone, something will know and my reward will fail.

Is it my fault family members are passing away?

The second to die was my Father – four of his brothers in a row, in twelve months eight relatives gone – this is domino... the last my nephew.

Seven die in ill health.

The eighth in the spell my nephew – except he ended the curse, he's missing – yes bothersome.

Missing is a gift – he politely stopped and spat on the spell – the curse in limbo as he cannot be found.

Human – blame the spirits if you have nowhere else to turn.

Am I so naive that I believe I have this ability – this influence to be scorned harmful energy?

It has been months since the Boy, my nephew, went missing in the river, they say.

My twenty-year-old nephew will always be the Boy.

To visit my sister and my brother-in-law was – I have no words, no short story, no poem, no earthling can articulate feelings I held.... I could not speak, I could not cry – disbelieve and why.

Tragedy.

I've said my peace, nothing more to tell – none of us know what happened. We've all been intercepted. The Boy is gone he has not been found.

Death by misadventure, if you are to die young, misadventure is a choice one could make.

You see... you've come into the story at the wrong time.

You will listen to the results.

I, the flawed, must live.

I should be in a shack I don't own – no job, just fun.

It isn't like this, I have two homes – I want nothing.

My Machine head says don't invest in sugar, sorrow, crooks, or charity after the fact.

I call reasoning 'Machine' to fit into the modern scheme of intelligence.

My wife says I'm smart – 'Smart for nothing'. A smart that is useless in the real world. I like it; I have no desire to be a function screw in the world built.

She can summon fire, surround me in flames, cool me in the sea.

Her and mine equal love and hate in this marriage.

'Why aren't you naked?' my wife asks. Don't you have to be naked when you get a massage?' she laughs.

No, not naked.

'Come on, take off your clothing – just leave your underwear on.'

Pale, what am I to do once I liked to be pale – before I didn't like pale skin – things change.

A tune up, is this what she is getting at.

Doesn't matter, my wife arranged and will pay the masseuse.

Everything that you expect a saint to be my wife is not – than again she is not Christian – she is no angel – she is not perfect – she is beyond what perfect should be – my Buddha, my teacher, my spiritual test. Her hair shines, her smile smirks away slight dishonesty – oh, but if you are on her side – the wicked is good, the lies funny, and the sly cool.

I don't care enough to lie; lie is to save yourself – I care enough to tell the truth; truth is hope to save oneself.

I have my faults – ruined any greatness early in my life – cannot undo the wrongs I've thought.

Diabolical – criminal – am I sick?

No, I'm incapable of sensibility. I believe in the unreal – the mind moves matter routine.

Labels are flexible, all parts of the human condition are in us – it is the attached label you must watch out for.

My wife tells the masseuse to stop.

The tune up is over.

I roll over to my stomach. She pays the masseuse – escorts her to the door.

We make love, installing memory to our skin that our minds absorb – goodbye children.

I'll miss this Cambodian puzzle

I'm going to Canada, Lake Wapa, British Columbia. The place I grew up.

My wife, relaxed and showered, is on the phone – speaking to her friends she loans money to, the collateral she's to keep, the payments she's to collect, six-month plans – two-week plans – business opportunities, she swears, talks loud – then calm. She laughs when she hears the answers she likes – she'll send our fourteen-year-old son to collect interest payments – or perhaps earnings from arrangements – she lends at a better rate than the bank. I don't listen – I won't see the money or lose the money I leave it to her . . .

I'm thinking of my flight to Canada, and how I'll neglect or fix my $120,000 debt.

Revolving earth.

Years ago, I was in Sri Lanka, swimming, writing, on my way to India. A friend owed me a minor debt – Cambodia I went instead of India to collect the debt.

I never thought wife – I thought visit friend, collect debt, and wonder at Khmer Temple Architecture.

I never did collect the debt – met my wife instead.

My wife says throw the thought of lost money away, if it wasn't for your friend we would have never met – sometimes the result of loss takes on a different form.

I have no strength to go to work – I have no plans to go to work, they've called and I've not answered, I have answered see you in the spring.

I have poetry and theory to attend.

I feel I still have jealousy – I still have how will I make money – I still have is my family safe – I still have should I continue to waste time and write or should I be working every minute of my life?

Should I have an affair?

If you do not live, what kind of poetry will it be? I want to go live in the trees find truth – or is it better to find truth in the city social every day? Both I say, to capture answers sought. Live it and reflect upon it.

Bank it.

What I know about death is nothing – I've never seen it – my wife has seen death, killing, massacre, covered the awful smell of death decay with clay.

She has a look of someone I've never met – a look that tells me she's been killed, lived, and will not be killed again.

A real story would be about her, not me.

She once told me, 'When you eat ants, they bite your tongue.'

How can I argue with that?

I'm not ready to face my story with her.

I'm facing alcohol today, jetlag and coffee tomorrow.

Mostly I'm to face family and friends – Christmas is near.

Also by Les Cook

About the Author

Travel experiences of the late 90s early 2000s became a novel.
Of course, the reality was more exciting than the book. You
must keep some things for yourself. – **Les Cook**

www.ingramcontent.com/pod-product-compliance
Lightning Source LLC
Chambersburg PA
CBHW052003170626
46808CB00007B/2757